Characters All at Sea!

by Jeremy Strong

Contents

Edinburgh Gate
Harlow, Essex

The Raft

When the ship sank Kim and Ben thought they would die. They clung to a piece of wood from the wreck. There were bits of broken ship all around them.

It was amazing that they had not drowned. Luckily both Ben and Kim could swim well. But it was easy to swim in a swimming pool. Now they were in the middle of the sea and the nearest land was a thousand miles away.

Kim hung on to the floating piece of wood. "What are we going to do?" she asked. Her voice sounded small and scared. Ben did not answer. He was looking around to see if there was something they could use to help them. But the storm was still making big waves. As soon as Ben thought he could see something, it would vanish behind a wave.

"Stay here," he shouted suddenly. "I think I can see something." Ben let go of the piece of wood and began to swim away. He fought his way through the waves. Yes! There it was! A big piece of deck from the boat, floating on the water. Ben struggled onto the deck. It would make a good raft. There was lots of room. He could even stand up on it.

Ben got to his feet and shouted across to Kim. "Over here," he cried. "I've found a raft that we can use."

Kim began to swim slowly across to the raft. Ben looked around to see what else he could find. Was there anything else floating in the water that might be useful to them? Yes! There was some rope, a plastic bowl, and there were some pieces of wood. Maybe they could use them as paddles. Maybe they could even make a little shelter on the raft. Ben grabbed the rope and the bowl before they sank.

Then he helped Kim onto the raft and she lay there, panting. He showed her what he had already found. Kim sat up. She shook her head sadly.

"Ben, we are going to need food and water. Where are we going get them from?"

Ben sat down next to her. She was right. Of course they would need food and water. He tried to sound brave and cheerful. "I'm sure we shall think of something. It's going to be all right."

Kim looked at him angrily. "I might be younger than you, Ben, but I'm not stupid," she snapped. "It's not going to be all right. We can float on this raft, but we need food and water to stay alive."

"People will come looking for us," said Ben. "There will be planes and helicopters. They'll spot us from the air. Maybe a boat will pass by and see us. Don't worry. Someone will save us, I'm sure."

Kim shook her head, but now Ben was getting cross. "We can't just give up," he said. "We must try to survive until we are saved. It's up to us, Kim. Come on, help me get this wood on board. Look, we can use this plastic bowl to collect rainwater to drink. Maybe we can try to catch some fish."

"We don't have anything to cook with," said Kim.

"Then if we catch some fish we shall have to eat them raw," Ben said.

"Ugh!" Kim pulled a face. "I am not going to eat raw fish!"

"Well, we can eat them raw, or we can die of hunger," said Ben. "Which would you prefer?"

The Biffaroo

"Listen to me," said the old sea captain. "You must never take a boat across Devil's Bay at night."

"Why not?" asked Kate.

"Because the Biffaroo will get you."

Kate laughed, but Max and Ziggy frowned.

"What is the Biffaroo?" asked Max.

"Do you mean to say that you have never heard of the Biffaroo?" cried the old sea captain. "Everyone round here knows about the Biffaroo."

"We're not from round here," Kate pointed out. "We live in Birmingham, not by the sea. We are here on holiday."

"Ah," growled the old sea captain. "Birmingham, eh? You are nothing but lily-livered landlubbers!"

"I bet you can't say that quickly," said Kate.

"Oh yes I can!" cried the old sea captain. "Lily-lubbered landlivers. I mean lubby-livered lilylanders. No, no, I mean rubby-dubby silly livers."

Kate was rolling about laughing. But Max and Ziggy still wanted to know what a Biffaroo was.

"Stop laughing and I will tell you," growled the old sea captain. "The Biffaroo is a sea monster. He lives out in the bay. He has a head like a giant cow."

"Which bit of a cow?" asked Kate. "The front bit, the back bit, or the bit underneath?"

"The front bit," snapped the old sea captain. "The monster

has a head like a cow's head. But he has very long, sharp teeth, like a snake's fangs."
"That doesn't sound very nice," said Ziggy, with a little shiver.

"It isn't very nice," said the old sea captain. "He has a very long neck, with fins down the back, like a dragon. The skin is all blotchy and yellow and green. The monster's body is long and fat. He has four legs. They are quite short, but they have huge, webbed feet and claws too. Each claw is like a dagger! I have seen men ripped to bits by those claws."
"Ugh!" said Max, and the old sea captain nodded.

"The Biffaroo has a tail too. It's as long and strong as a python. It could squeeze the life out of you." The captain grinned. "I have seen men squashed to jelly by that tail."

"Ugh!" said Ziggy, and the old sea captain nodded again.

"At the end of the tail there is a big, round, knobbly bit, with great spikes sticking out of it. I have seen men crushed like ants by that big round knobbly bit."

Lily-livered land lubbers!

Ziggy and Max had turned white. Their eyes were as round as dinner plates. But Kate just laughed.

"I don't believe you," she said. "You are making this up. There is no such thing as the Biffaroo. You are just trying to scare us."

"He **has** scared us!" cried Max and Ziggy.

"Well he hasn't scared me!" cried Kate bravely. "Tonight I am going to take the boat out across Devil's Bay. Then you will see that here is no such thing as the Biffaroo."

The old sea captain grabbed Kate by the arm. "Don't you go out there!" he cried. "There are terrible things out there, waiting for you."

"You can't stop me," said Kate. "I shall go out there and show you that there is nothing to be scared of."

Late that night Kate climbed into a small rowing boat. She set out across Devil's Bay. The pale moon shone upon the

water and made the waves glitter. Max and Ziggy watched her from the beach.

"It's all right," she shouted back to them. "I told you there was no monster."

At that very moment, the sea began to boil. Great bubbles burst on the surface. The boat began to rock about. Kate was almost thrown into the water. Even the moon hid behind a cloud. There was something huge beneath the waves. It was coming up to the surface. Closer and closer it came until Kate could see a giant shadow just below the waves.

A Nightmare Journey

I shall never forget that ferry crossing. Four of us were travelling back to England from France. We had our two children with us, Daniel and Jessica. We had just finished a wonderful holiday, camping in different parts of France. Now we were ready to make our journey home.

We drove all day, towing our trailer-tent behind us. We must have travelled a good five hundred miles to reach the French port of Calais. The roads were nice and clear. It was a good journey. But as soon as we reached Calais – disaster! There were huge queues of cars and lorries and coaches waiting to drive onto the ferries. But there was a problem. There were no ferries!

The weather in the English Channel had turned nasty. The sea was very rough. The ferries were taking a long time to make the crossing, and it was difficult for them to dock when they reached the harbour.

We waited our turn in the queue. We felt nervous and a bit worried. We had finished our holiday and now we just wanted to get home. But we didn't want to sail across such a rough sea!

It was a long wait, but we had our camping things with us. We got out our stove and put the kettle on to boil. We cooked our supper. We sat and read and listened to the car radio.

"There are strong gales in the English Channel this evening," said the weather forecast. "Many channel ferry services have been cancelled. Only a few ferries are still running, and they are fighting the dreadful weather." That weather report didn't make us feel any better!

At last, after waiting eight hours, the queue began to go down. It was another three hours before it was our turn to drive onto the ferry. We sat in the car on the dockside, watching with everyone else as the giant ferry tried to dock. The waves were huge, even inside the harbour. The big ferry would try to dock and then the crashing waves would lift it away. It tried again and again, and each time the waves stopped it from docking.

At last the ferry made it. A big cheer went up from all the people waiting to get on board. But our problems were only just beginning. When we drove on board we saw the sailors tying the lorries and coaches to the deck with huge chains. It was to stop them moving about once we had set sail.

"It looks like the crew are expecting trouble," my wife said to me quietly.

"What are those big chains for?" Daniel asked.

"It's to keep them safe," I said, and I tried to sound cheerful. "They always do that with lorries and coaches." But I knew they didn't. The crew only tied them down when there was a really rough sea.

Once the ferry had safely loaded up, it set sail for England. Up and down went the boat, and it was still inside the harbour! As soon as we passed out between the harbour walls the full strength of the storm hit us. It felt just as if the ferry kept hitting a solid brick wall. The bow at the front of the ship was lifted high into the air as giant waves passed beneath it. Then the bow would come crashing down and hit the next wave head on.

As well as crashing up and down, the ferry rolled from side to side. People began to be seasick. Children were crying. People were staggering about. They could hardly stay on their feet. They clung to railings, curtains, each other, anything. Plates and glasses and cutlery spilled to the floor and broke.

It was a nightmare journey.

The Indoor Pirates

The Indoor Pirates lived at Number 25, Dolphin Street. They did not want anyone to know that they lived there, so they took the number off the front door. Then they hung a skull-and-crossbones flag from the chimney-pot. Of course, all the neighbours knew at once that they had pirates living near them, but they didn't mind, because the pirates stayed indoors most of the time. (That was how they got their name.)

The leader of the Indoor Pirates was Captain Blackpatch. He really did have a patch too, although it was not over one eye. It was on the sleeve of his jacket where he had torn it on a nail. His grandparents had been pirates. His mother and father had been pirates. It seemed obvious that he should be a pirate too. This was just a little unfortunate, because Blackpatch hated the sea. In fact, he hated water of any kind – drinking water, bath-water, washing-up water – and most of all sea-water. Blackpatch wished he didn't have to go on boats at all.

One day he got a letter from his great-grandmother, who was very old. She was 107, and she had patches too. There was one on her dress, one on her leather smoking jacket (she loved big cigars), and another on her thumb where she had cut it by mistake. It was quite a nasty cut, and it made Great-granny realise that she was getting too old to look after herself properly. She wanted her great-grandson to come home and see to her needs. The letter made Blackpatch very happy. At last he could live on dry land!

Off he went, and he looked after Great-granny very well until she died. (By this time she was 112.) Great-granny left her house to Blackpatch, saying that she hoped he would look after it, and the first thing that Blackpatch did was to write a letter of his own. He wrote to all his friends at sea – all the ones who didn't like it – and he asked them to come and live with him at Number 25, Dolphin Street. And that was how the Indoor Pirates began.

25 Dolphin Street
Dear Blackpatch,
I am now 107
and need some
help. I can't light
my cigars by myself
anymore. Come
home please.
Love
Great Granny
Blackpatch
xx
P.S. Bring some
more matches

First of all there was Bald Ben. He had huge muscles and was immensely strong. He could lift up two people at once, one under each arm. He hadn't a single hair on his bald head. Instead, right in the middle, he had a colourful tattoo of a rose, with I LOVE MUM written underneath. Bald Ben didn't like going to sea because it meant missing too much television.

Polly and Molly were twin sisters. They looked just like each other, except that Polly's hair was bunched out by her right ear, and Molly's was bunched by her left ear. They were always, ALWAYS arguing with each other. Whatever one said, the other said the opposite, even if it was nonsense.

"We're sisters," Polly might say. "No we're not!" Molly would snap. "We're ..." and she would screw up her eyes desperately, "... brothers!" "You're stupid," Polly would answer.

"You're the one that's stupid," Molly would reply, and so it would go on. The twins didn't like going to sea because they couldn't swim.

The fifth and last Indoor Pirate was Lumpy Lawson. He didn't look lumpy at all – in fact he was tall and rather skinny with it. Lumpy Lawson did all the cooking and whenever he made porridge there were gigantic stodgy lumps in it. That was how he got his name. He didn't like going on boats because if he tried to make soup at sea it always slopped over the top of the pan. The boiling soup splattered onto his feet and that made him leap about shouting very, VERY bad words like "Jigglepoops!"

From *The Indoor Pirates* by Jeremy Strong

The Lost Vikings

Through the mist came the creak of many oars. Now and then there was a splash. The grey mist swirled and slid over the flat, grey sea, but not a sign could be seen of the boats; only the steady slap of oars and a few low curses.

Then a dark shadow moved within the mist, growing blacker as it came nearer. The great wooden hulk of a Viking war-boat appeared, trailing wisps of fog along its sides. Twenty oars bit into the water, and forty Viking warriors strained over the heavy poles.

"Never have I seen a fog like this," hissed the leader. He was a tall Dane, with a huge moustache and a fiery red beard. "There is something I do not like about it." He cast a glance at the lookout, standing up by the great dragon-head prow. "Is there no sign of the fleet? Where are the other boats?"

The lookout sucked one finger and held it up, as if to judge the wind direction. He stared into the mist, took off his helmet and pulled out both ears like radar scanners. His ears were big and red. The Viking leader cursed.

"Sigurd is an idiot. Why do we use a fool for a lookout?" Beside him, Tostig laughed.

"It's quite simple, Ulric. Sigurd can't row or cook. What else is there for him to do? You know what happened the last time he was at the oars. We ended up going round in a circle for almost an hour. And when he was cook, he boiled all our best meat in a pot of sea-water. Ugh! At least he's safe up there."

Ulric Blacktooth spat. "Look at him, holding out his ears. What a fool!" He shouted forward. "What can you see, Sigurd?"

"There's a lot of mist about," answered the lookout. "No, no, wait, there's something else. I can see something else through the mist!"

Ulric Blacktooth gripped the mast. Had they found the rest of the war-party at last? "What is it? What can you see?"

"Wait a minute, the mist is clearing. Yes! I can see it quite clearly now."

“What is it, what is it?” bellowed Ulric impatiently.

“There’s water below, Ulric. I can see water. It’s – the sea!”

Ulric Blacktooth shut his eyes and banged his head several times against the ship’s mast. “Tostig,” he hissed, “that man will be the death of us all. Why are we cursed with such a fool?”

Tostig was snorting through his nose, a sure sign that he was losing his temper. Temper-losing was something that Tostig was very good at. He did it quite often – and practice makes perfect. Now he drew his sword, which he had named Heartsplitter, and strode forward. In a moment he was beside the lookout.

“Sigurd, of course you can see the sea. We are on a boat. We are at sea.” Tostig spoke as if he wanted each word to hit Sigurd like a hammer. “Now, Sigurd, if you wish to stay alive, do something useful! Get yourself up that dragon’s head, sit on top and don’t say a word until you see the English coast. Do you hear?”

So saying, Tostig thrust his sword (the pointed end) very close to Sigurd’s backside. Sigurd gave a yelp and a jump and scuttled up the prow, until he was right on the dragon’s head. From there, he turned and looked back at Tostig.

“I was only trying to help,” he complained.

Tostig grunted and returned to Ulric, while Sigurd sighed and tried very hard to see through all the mist that surrounded them. He was bored and tired. He had been on lookout duty for days. For some strange reason, nobody would let him row. Sigurd had always thought rowing was his best subject.

The boat was part of a large Viking raiding fleet, headed for England. They had been at sea for seven days, and the mist had been with them for the last twenty-four hours. It was a creepy, evil mist, making everyone nervous and jumpy. Somehow they had become separated from the rest of the fleet. Now they were drifting, they knew not where.

Sigurd strained his eyes to see through the mist. He pricked up his ears. What was that? Could he hear something? Was it the sound of breakers on the shore? Sigurd perched as far forward as possible, lying across the dragon's nose. He thought of shouting to Ulric and Tostig, but they'd only be cross.

From *There's a Viking in my Bed!* by Jeremy Strong

Sir Rupert and Rosie

The wind was fresh and clean and whipped spray from the sea in silver puffs of glittering stars. Several dolphins had joined the ship and for the last hour had been leaping and rolling just ahead of The Lame Duck's dipping prow. Rosie and Nanny leaned over one side of the ship, watching them. Sir Rupert leaned over the other side, being sick.

"I reckon that if ever I die and I'm reincarnated I'll come back as a dolphin," mused Nanny.
"What does 'reincarnation' mean?" Rosie asked.
"Well now, my pretty piglet, it's what some people think will happen after you die. They reckon that afterwards you come back as another life-form. Most people want to come back as someone rich or famous ..." Nanny paused and watched the glistening curved backs of the dolphins. "... But I think I'd rather be a dolphin."
"Do you think it's true?" Rosie's freckled nose had several thoughtful wrinkles on it.
"Ooh, who can say? Nobody's ever died and come back to tell us."

Rosie smiled and gazed up at the fresh sky and flying clouds. "I think I'd like to be a bird – a seagull – or maybe an albatross." Sir Rupert came staggering across the deck, and grasped the rails next to his daughter.
"I'm dying," he groaned.
"Ooh dear me," said Nanny, winking at Rosie. "And if you do die, Sir Rupert, which I'm sure I hope you won't, what would you like to come back as?"
"A lump of rock," heaved Sir Rupert.

Rosie and Nanny frowned. “And why would you be wanting to be a rock then?” Nanny couldn’t resist asking.
“Because,” hiccuped the brave explorer, “rocks don’t do anything. Rocks don’t feel anything. Rocks don’t have to go on dangerous missions. They don’t get ill. They don’t get seasick. They don’t **think**, they don’t **do**, they’re just – rocks.” Sir Rupert’s stomach lurched and heaved once more. When it was over, he slithered to the deck in a sad heap, muttering

to himself. “I want to be a rock. Just a small one will do nicely. I’m not ambitious.”

“Pirates,” muttered Muggins. “Could be pirates, Cap’n, come to steal our gold.”
“Whoever it is, they do look as if they’re spoiling for a fight,” Rosie said, and the crew began whispering darkly to the First Mate.
“I can’t believe a tiny tub like that would want to fight us,” murmured Sir Rupert.

“’Scuse me, Cap’n,” Muggins interrupted, “but the crew say if there’s going to be a fight can we make sail and run away?” Rosie was outraged.
“Muggins! You’re supposed to be brave sailors!”
“Ah yes Miss, an’ that we are too. We ’ave the bravest hearts on the Six Seas ...”
“Seven ...” muttered Sir Rupert weakly.
“... bravest hearts on the Seven Seas. It’s just our legs that aren’t so brave you see, an’ they do so like to go in the opposite direction.”

How long this discussion would have gone on for is impossible to say, for they were rudely interrupted by the loud boom of a cannon, and moments later a fountain of water spouted from the sea just ahead of The Lame Duck. In an instant the dolphins dived and vanished. If those strange humans were going to start throwing big lumpy things at each other again, they didn't want to know.

From *Sir Rupert and Rosie Gussett in Deadly Danger* by Jeremy Strong